With the most humble of hearts for the blessing of such a caring and supportive family and upbringing, I dedicate this book to my late grandfather, Nathaniel Jones.

I also want to express such gratefulness to all of my loving family. I am so thankful to each member—from the oldest to the youngest—for teaching me the true meaning of family, unconditional support, and for always believing in me, my dreams, and the endeavors life brings my way.

Thank you,
Chris

To my sons, Nyree, Tyreek, and Nasir. Never stop dreaming. They eventually come true.—F. M.

SIMON & SCHUSTER BOOKS FOR YOUNG READERS
An imprint of Simon & Schuster Children's Publishing Division
1230 Avenue of the Americas, New York, New York 10020
Text copyright © 2009 by Chris Paul
Illustrations copyright © 2009 by Frank Morrison
All rights reserved, including the right of reproduction in whole or in part in any form.
SIMON & SCHUSTER BOOKS FOR YOUNG READERS is a trademark of Simon & Schuster, Inc.
Book design by Lucy Ruth Cummins
The text for this book is set in Kosmik and Plz Print Brush.
The illustrations for this book are rendered in acrylic.
Manufactured in China
2 4 6 8 10 9 7 5 3
Library of Congress Cataloging-in-Publication Data
Paul, Chris.
Long shot : never too small to dream big / Chris Paul ; illustrated by Frank Morrison.—1st ed.
p. cm.
Summary: Although he is shorter than most of his classmates and everyone discourages him from trying out for the basketball team, eight-year-old Chris just works harder than everyone else so his size will not matter.
ISBN: 978-1-4169-5079-0
[1. Basketball—Fiction. 2. Size—Fiction. 3. Persistence—Fiction.]
I. Morrison, Frank, 1971- ill. II. Title.
PZ7.P2783425Lo 2009
[E]—dc22
2008035758

LONG SHOT

NEVER TOO SMALL TO DREAM BIG

CHRIS PAUL

Illustrated by FRANK MORRISON

Simon & Schuster Books for Young Readers
New York London Toronto Sydney

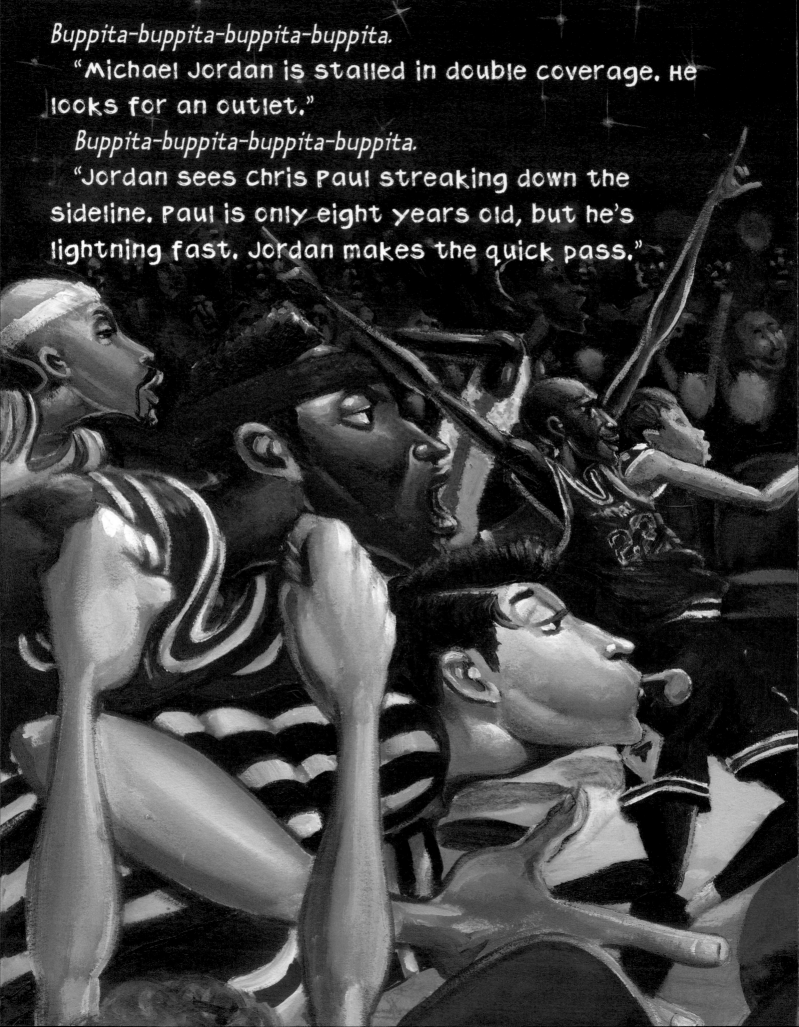

Buppita-buppita-buppita-buppita.

"Michael Jordan is stalled in double coverage. He looks for an outlet."

Buppita-buppita-buppita-buppita.

"Jordan sees Chris Paul streaking down the sideline. Paul is only eight years old, but he's lightning fast. Jordan makes the quick pass."

Buppita-buppita-buppita-buppita.
"Paul drives left, pulls back for the jumper. He lets it go—and scores! The crowd goes wild!"

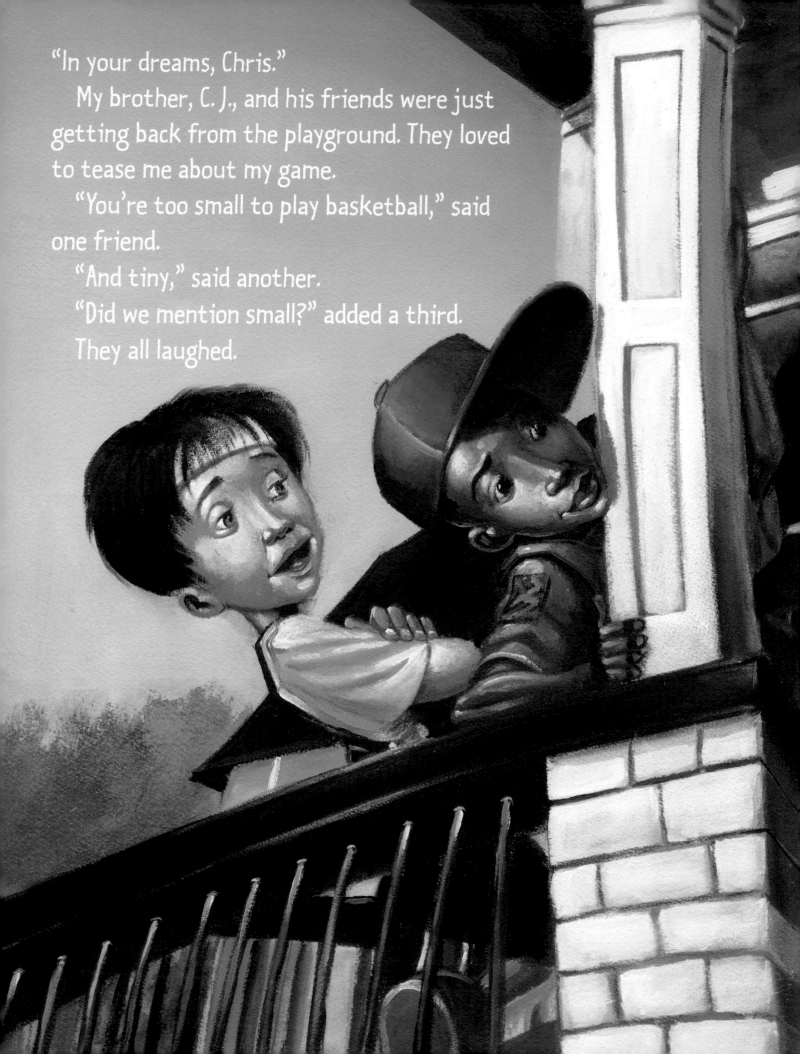

"In your dreams, Chris."

My brother, C. J., and his friends were just getting back from the playground. They loved to tease me about my game.

"You're too small to play basketball," said one friend.

"And tiny," said another.

"Did we mention small?" added a third.

They all laughed.

C. J. stayed behind as his friends left.

"They're right, you know, Chris," he said. "The ball is bigger than you are."

I threw back my shoulders and straightened up.

"Maybe," I said. "But I've got good hands. Come on, help me practice. Tryouts are only a week away."

"Hey," called our mother from the doorway. "What you boys need to practice is setting the table and eating your vegetables. Basketball will still be there after supper."

At school the next day I didn't pay much attention. All I could think about were the tryouts.

When my teacher talked about math, I remembered that the average height of a player in the NBA was 6 feet 7 inches tall. I was only 4 feet 1 inch tall. And I wasn't going to get much taller in the next few days.

That night I was lying in bed when Mom came in.

"What are you thinking about, Chris?"

"Coach is only going to take fifteen players. What if he thinks I'm too small?"

Mom smiled. "You're a great basketball player, Chris. But basketball isn't the only thing that matters. Your family matters. Your education does too. And worrying about your height won't make you any better. Just do the best you can with the gifts you have."

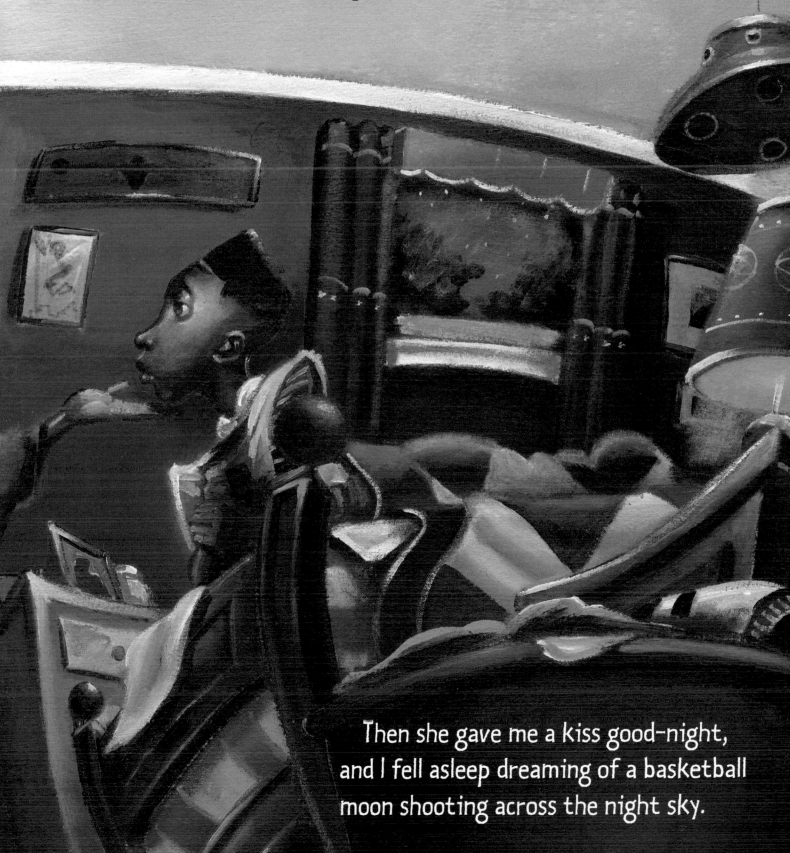

Then she gave me a kiss good-night, and I fell asleep dreaming of a basketball moon shooting across the night sky.

But I was still feeling scared on Saturday when I helped out my grandfather, Papa Chilly, at his service station.

"You look a little deflated yourself," said Papa Chilly as I filled a flat tire. "What's up?"

"Everyone says I'm too small to make the basketball team," I said.

"Nothing wrong with being nervous," said Papa Chilly. "Look, Chris, you can't make yourself taller, but you can get faster and stronger." He winked at me. "Work harder then everyone else on the court and your size won't matter."

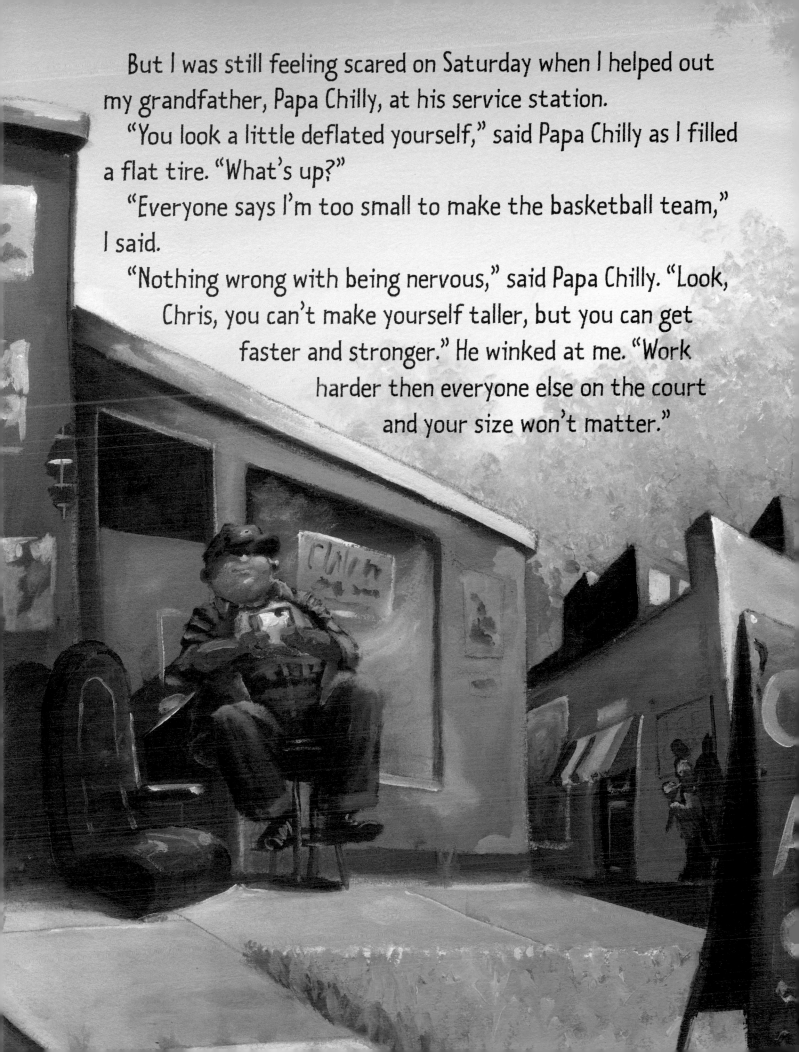

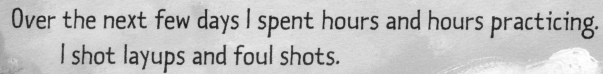

Over the next few days I spent hours and hours practicing.
I shot layups and foul shots.
I dribbled first with one hand and then with the other.
I ran sprints to build up my wind.

One day my brother came out onto the driveway, where I was resting. "Hey, squirt!" said C. J. "I've been watching you."

"Really?" I didn't know C. J. ever watched me.

"Yeah, well, don't tell anyone," said C. J. "But listen, when you drive to the basket, don't look at the ball. Your hand should know where the ball is without looking."

I nodded.

"And when somebody tries to fake you out, don't watch their arms or their head. Keep your eye on their hips. Nobody goes anywhere without their hips."

The night before the tryouts, I could hardly eat.

"Try to relax, Chris," said Dad. "You're a good player."

"He isn't worried about being good," said C. J. "He's worried about being short."

"It's true," I said. "What if the coach makes up his mind about me before I even play?"

My father shook his head. "A good coach will want to see what you're made of."

"And remember," Mom added, "you're not alone in this. The whole family is behind you."

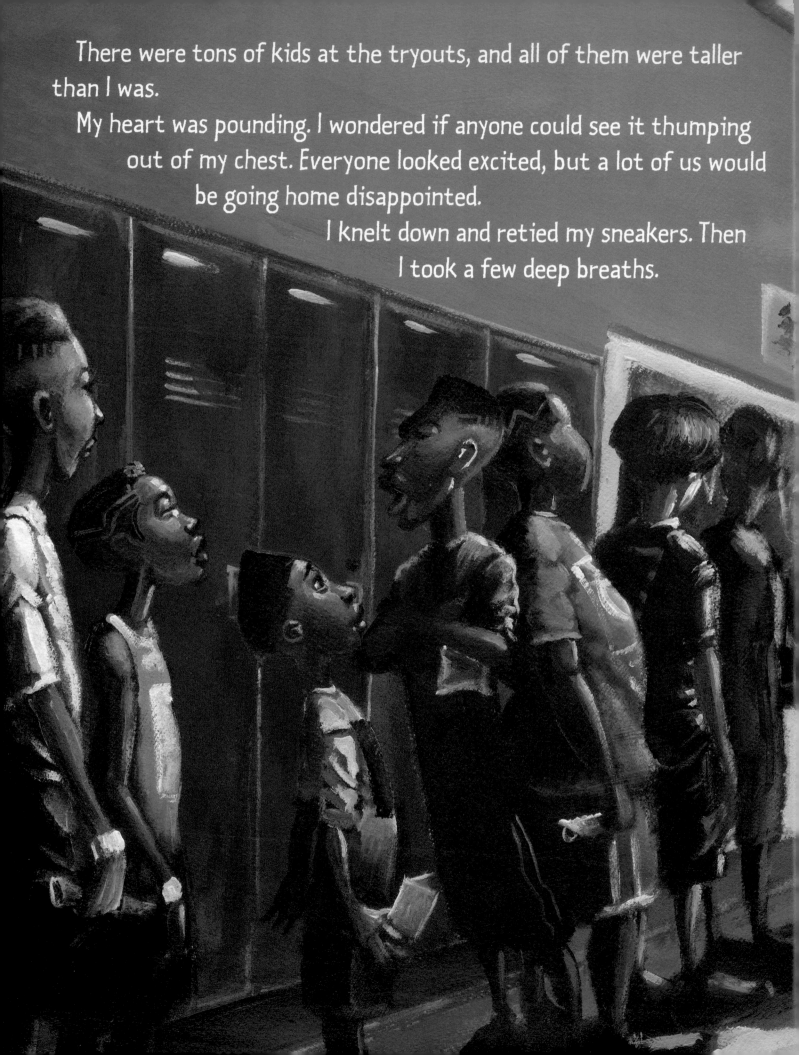

There were tons of kids at the tryouts, and all of them were taller than I was.

My heart was pounding. I wondered if anyone could see it thumping out of my chest. Everyone looked excited, but a lot of us would be going home disappointed.

I knelt down and retied my sneakers. Then I took a few deep breaths.

The coach split us into several teams. When my team took the court, I got the inbounds pass. I dribbled upcourt. The opposing guard watched the ball closely. Too closely. I faked a pass right—and then went left for an open shot.

Swish!

"Good move, Chris!" yelled Dad.

I got the ball back after the next basket, and the defense boxed me in. I forced a shot, but it was swatted away and I was knocked to the ground.

"Careful, don't step on him!" somebody shouted from the sidelines.

I was done—I could feel it. I didn't dare look at the coach, but I heard Papa Chilly cheering from the stands. He didn't think I was done. He thought I was just getting started.

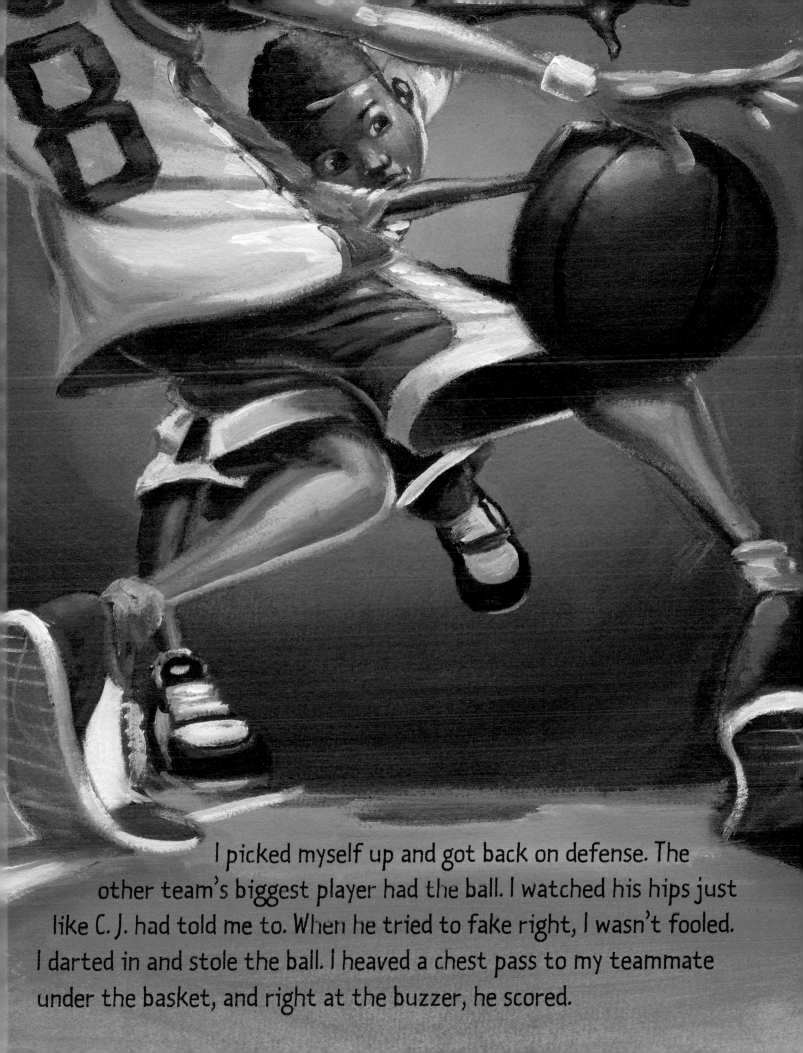

I picked myself up and got back on defense. The other team's biggest player had the ball. I watched his hips just like C. J. had told me to. When he tried to fake right, I wasn't fooled. I darted in and stole the ball. I heaved a chest pass to my teammate under the basket, and right at the buzzer, he scored.

Afterward we all waited for the big decision. The coach sat by himself for a few minutes, looking at his notes. Then he stood up and came forward.

"You all looked great today," he said. "Everyone should be proud of that."

I held my breath.

"So here's our team for the coming season."

The coach named three centers. Then the six forwards. That left six more spaces for guards.

I wasn't the first player named. Or the second. Three more names went by. There was only one left. What if it wasn't me?

"... and Chris Paul!"
the coach finished up.

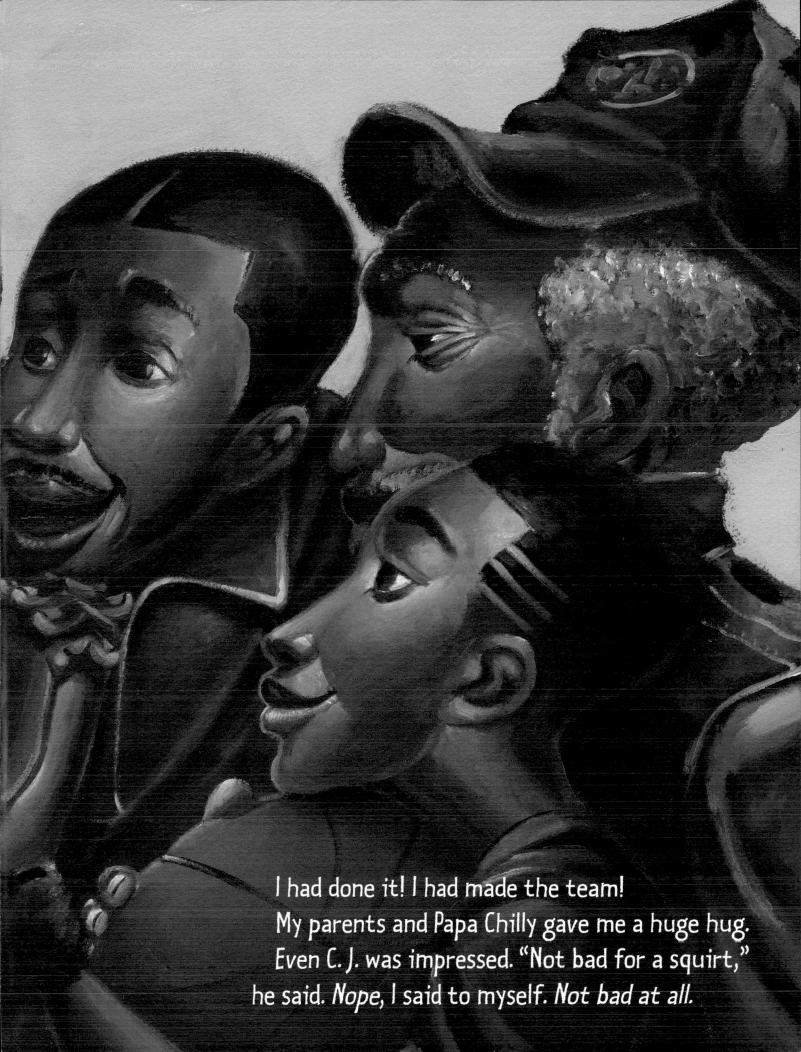

I had done it! I had made the team!
My parents and Papa Chilly gave me a huge hug.
Even C. J. was impressed. "Not bad for a squirt,"
he said. *Nope*, I said to myself. *Not bad at all.*

All About NBA Superstar Chris Paul

Chris Paul's rise to the NBA began on the courts of West Forsyth High School in Winston-Salem, North Carolina, where he led the Titans to the state Class 4A Eastern Regional Final and a record of 27-3 during his senior year. Arguably one of the most significant moments in his basketball career came when, as a senior, he tallied 61 points in one game in honor of his grandfather, Nathaniel Jones, a.k.a. Papa Chilly, who was tragically murdered just days before. When Chris reached the 61-point mark (his grandfather was 61 years old), he intentionally missed a free throw, then took himself out of the game in a fitting tribute to the man who meant so much to him.

Chris chose to stay close to home for college and starred on the basketball team at Wake Forest University, where he went on to become a two-time All-American.

Now in the NBA, Chris has emerged as the unquestionable leader of the New Orleans Hornets and the face of the franchise. Chris finished second in the regular season MVP balloting and was named an NBA All-Star for the first time in 2008 after leading the Hornets in scoring with 21.1 points per game. His 2.71 steals per game and 11.6 assists per game were tops in the league as well. Chris also guided the Hornets to their first Southwest Division title in franchise history.

During his second season, Chris led the Hornets in assists, steals, and total points and was a member of the sophomore squad at the 2007 T-Mobile Rookie Challenge & Youth Jam at the NBA's All-Star Weekend.

Chris was also a member of the 2008 USA Olympic team, which took home the gold medal.